Hello Kitty®'s

The New Friend

By Elizabeth Bennett
Illustrated by Sachiho Hino

SCHOLASTIC INC.

ISBN 978-0-545-55421-3

12 11 10 9 8 7 6 5 4 3   13 14 15 16 17 18/0

Printed in the U.S.A.   40

This edition first printing, March 2013

🐱 and 🐱 got off the 🚐.

🐱 was waiting for them.

🐱 wanted to know how 🏫 was that day.

The day was okay. But 🐱 hoped tomorrow would be better.

Their teacher, , had promised there would be a new girl in their class tomorrow, and their class would be getting a .

When it was time for 🛏 ,

🐱 read 🐱 and 🐱

a 📘 .

🐱 looked at the 🕐

and turned out the light.

🐱 wished them a good night

as 🐱 closed her 👁 👁 .

After a yummy breakfast

of 🥞 and 🥛,

🐱 grabbed her 🎒

and ran to catch the 🚌.

🐱 got on the 🚌, too.

🐱 found a seat next to

her friend 🐑.

They talked about the new

girl at 🏫.

 put away her and put her on her .

 rang the .

 introduced the class to the new girl. Her name was Connie.

sat at an empty next to .

looked at with a big smile on her face.

Mimmy · Hello Kitty · Tippy · Fifi · Thom

At lunchtime,  looked

for .

They ate lunch together every day.

 couldn't believe her 👁 👁.

 was sitting with 🐼 and

there was no room for  at

the lunch 🛎.

She ate her lunch and drank

her 🥛 by herself.

 went to the playground.

Sometimes she and 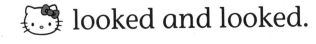 played

 at recess.

Sometimes they went on

the .

Where was ?

 looked and looked.

Finally she saw her. was

sitting by the big .

She was talking to .

Tippy and Joey were there, too.

did not go over to them.

Her friends were busy with .

They weren't looking for .

 felt sad.

She thought it would be fun

to have a new girl in , but

she wasn't having fun.

She missed .

 looked at the on the wall.

She couldn't wait for the

to ring.

At home, told about .

All their friends had played with .

No one played with .

 gave the girls and .

 wondered why didn't ask

to join her friends.

 couldn't think of a good reason.

The next morning, 🐱 put on her 🎒 and climbed onto the 🚐. 🐑 had saved a seat for 🐱. 🐱 looked down the row. She saw a seat for her right between 🐑 and 🐄. Now 🐱 was happy to see her best friend . . . and her new friend!

Did you spot all the picture clues in this Hello Kitty book?

Each picture clue is on a flash card. Ask a grown-up to cut out the flash cards. Then try reading the words on the back of the cards. The pictures will be your clue.

Reading is fun with Hello Kitty!

Mimmy	Hello Kitty
Mama	school
hamster	Mr. Bearly

Papa	bed
clock	book
pancakes	eyes

backpack	milk
Fifi	bus
bell	desk

table	Connie
swing	ball
cookies	tree